A Christmas Sermon

Robert Louis Stevenson

Contents

A CHRISTMAS SERMON

BY

Robert Louis Stevenson

A CHRISTMAS SERMON

By the time this paper appears, I shall have been talking for twelve months;[1] and it is thought I should take my leave in a formal and seasonable manner. Valedictory eloquence is rare, and death-bed sayings have not often hit the mark of the occasion. Charles Second, wit and sceptic, a man whose life had been one long lesson in human incredulity, an easy-going comrade, a manoeuvring king--remembered and embodied all his wit and scepticism along with more than his usual good humour in the famous "I am afraid, gentlemen, I am an unconscionable time a-dying."

[Note 1: i.e. In the pages of ***Scribner's Magazine*** (1888).]

I

An unconscionable time a-dying--there is the picture ("I am afraid, gentlemen,") of your life and of mine. The sands run out, and the hours are "numbered and imputed," and the days go by; and when the last of these finds us, we have been a long time dying, and what else? The very length is something, if we reach that hour of separation undishonoured; and to have lived at all is doubtless (in the soldierly expression) to have served. There is a tale in Tacitus of how the veterans mutinied in the German wilderness; of how they mobbed Germanicus, clamouring to go home; and of how, seizing their general's hand, these old, war-worn exiles passed his finger along their toothless gums. Sunt lacrymae rerum: this was the most eloquent of the songs of Simeon. And when a man has lived to a fair age, he bears his marks of service. He may have never been remarked upon the breach at the head of the army; at least he shall have lost his teeth on the camp bread.

The idealism of serious people in this age of ours is of a noble character. It never seems to them that they have served enough; they have a fine impatience of their virtues. It were perhaps more modest to be singly thankful that we are no worse. It is not only our enemies, those desperate characters--it is we ourselves who know not what we do;--thence springs the glimmering hope that perhaps we do better than we think: that to scramble through this random business with hands reasonably clean, to have played the part of a man or woman with some reasonable fulness, to have often resisted the diabolic, and at the end to be still resisting it, is for the poor human soldier to have done right well. To ask to see some fruit of our endeavour is but a transcendental way of serving for reward; and what we take to be contempt of self is only greed of hire.

And again if we require so much of ourselves, shall we not require much of others? If we do not genially judge our own deficiencies, is it not to be feared we shall be even stern to the trespasses of others? And he who (looking back upon his own life) can see no more than that he has been unconscionably long a-dying, will he not be tempted to think his neighbour unconscionably long of getting hanged? It is probable that nearly all who think of conduct at all, think of it too much; it is certain we all think too much of sin. We are not damned for doing wrong, but for not doing right; Christ would never hear of negative morality; ***thou shalt*** was ever his word, with which he superseded thou shalt not. To make our idea of morality centre on forbidden acts is to defile the imagination and to introduce into our judgments of our fellow-men a secret element of gusto. If a thing is wrong for us, we should not dwell upon the thought of it; or we shall soon dwell upon it with inverted pleasure. If we cannot drive it from our minds--one thing of two: either our creed is in the wrong and we must more indulgently remodel it; or else, if our morality be in the right, we are criminal lunatics and should place our persons in restraint. A mark of such unwholesomely divided minds is the passion for interference with others: the Fox without the Tail was of this breed, but had (if his biographer is to be trusted) a certain antique civility now out of date. A man may have a flaw, a weakness, that unfits him for the duties of life, that spoils his temper, that threatens his integrity, or that betrays him into cruelty. It has to be conquered; but it must never be suffered to engross his thoughts. The true duties lie all upon the farther side, and must be attended to with a whole mind so soon as this preliminary clearing of the decks has been effected. In order that he may be kind and honest, it may be needful he should become a total abstainer; let him become so then, and the next day let him forget the circumstance. Trying to be kind and honest will require all his thoughts; a mortified appetite is never a wise companion; in so far as he has had to mortify an appetite, he will still be the worse man; and of such an one a great deal of cheerfulness will be required in judging life, and a great deal of humility in judging others.

It may be argued again that dissatisfaction with our life's endeavour springs in some degree from dulness. We require higher tasks, because we do not recognise the height of those we have. Trying to be kind and honest seems an affair too simple and too inconsequential for gentlemen of our heroic mould; we had rather set ourselves to something bold, arduous, and conclusive; we had rather found a schism or suppress a heresy, cut off a hand or mortify an appetite. But the task before us, which is to co-endure with our existence, is rather one of microscopic fineness, and the heroism required is that of patience. There is no cutting of the Gordian knots of life; each must be smilingly unravelled.

To be honest, to be kind--to earn a little and to spend a little less, to make upon the whole a family happier for his presence, to renounce when that shall be necessary and not be embittered, to keep a few friends but these without capitulation--above all, on the same grim condition, to keep friends with himself--here is a task for all that a man has of fortitude and delicacy. He has an ambitious soul who would ask more; he has a hopeful spirit who should look in such an enterprise to be successful. There is indeed one element in human destiny that not blindness itself can controvert: whatever else we are intended to do, we are not intended to succeed; failure is the fate allotted. It is so in every art and study; it is so above all in the continent art of living well. Here is a pleasant thought for the year's end or for the end of life: Only self-deception will be satisfied, and there need be no despair for the despairer.

II

But Christmas is not only the mile-mark of another year, moving us to thoughts of self-examination: it is a season, from all its associations, whether domestic or religious, suggesting thoughts of joy. A man dissatisfied with his endeavours is a man tempted to sadness. And in the midst of the winter, when his life runs lowest and he is reminded of the empty chairs of his beloved, it is well he should be condemned to this fashion of the smiling face. Noble disappointment, noble self-denial are not to be admired, not even to be pardoned, if they bring bitterness. It is one thing to enter the kingdom of heaven maim; another to maim yourself and stay without. And the kingdom of heaven is of the childlike, of those who are easy to please, who love and who give pleasure. Mighty men of their hands, the smiters and the builders and the judges, have lived long and done sternly and yet preserved this lovely character; and among our carpet interests and twopenny concerns, the shame were indelible if ***we*** should lose it. Gentleness and cheerfulness, these come before all morality; they are the perfect duties. And it is the trouble with moral men that they have neither one nor other. It was the moral man, the Pharisee, whom Christ could not away with. If your morals make you dreary, depend upon it they are wrong. I do not say "give them up," for they may be all you have; but conceal them like a vice, lest they should spoil the lives of better and simpler people.

A strange temptation attends upon man: to keep his eye on pleasures, even when he will not share in them; to aim all his morals against them. This very year a lady (singular iconoclast!) proclaimed a crusade against dolls; and the racy sermon against lust is a feature of the age.

I venture to call such moralists insincere. At any excess or perversion of a natural appetite, their lyre sounds of itself with relishing denunciations; but for all displays of the truly diabolic--envy, malice, the mean lie, the mean silence, the calumnious truth, the backbiter, the petty tyrant, the peevish poisoner of family life--their standard is quite different. These are wrong, they will admit, yet somehow not so wrong; there is no zeal in their assault on them, no secret element of gusto warms up the sermon; it is for things not wrong in themselves that they reserve the choicest of their indignation. A man may naturally disclaim all moral kinship with the Reverend Mr. Zola or the hobgoblin old lady of the dolls; for these are gross and naked instances. And yet in each of us some similar element resides. The sight of a pleasure in which we cannot or else will not share moves us to a particular impatience. It may be because we are envious, or because we are sad, or because we dislike noise and romping--being so refined, or because--being so philosophic--we have an overweighing sense of life's gravity: at least, as we go on in years, we are all tempted to frown upon our neighbour's pleasures. People are nowadays so fond of resisting temptations; here is one to be resisted. They are fond of self-denial; here is a propensity that cannot be too peremptorily denied. There is an idea abroad among moral people that they should make their neighbours good. One person I have to make good: myself. But my duty to my neighbour is much more nearly expressed by saying that I have to make him happy--if I may.

III

Happiness and goodness, according to canting moralists, stand in the relation of effect and cause. There was never anything less proved or less probable: our happiness is never in our own hands; we inherit our constitution; we stand buffet among friends and enemies; we may be so built as to feel a sneer or an aspersion with unusual keenness, and so circumstanced as to be unusually exposed to them; we may have nerves very sensitive to pain, and be afflicted with a disease very painful. Virtue will not help us, and it is not meant to help us. It is not even its own reward, except for the self-centred and--I had almost said--the unamiable. No man can pacify his conscience; if quiet be what he want, he shall do better to let that organ perish from disuse. And to avoid the penalties of the law, and the minor ***capitis diminutio*** of social ostracism, is an affair of wisdom--of cunning, if you will--and not of virtue.

In his own life, then, a man is not to expect happiness, only to profit by it gladly when it shall arise; he is on duty here; he knows not how or why, and does not need to know; he knows not for what hire, and must not ask. Somehow or other, though he does not know what goodness is, he must try to be good; somehow or other, though he cannot tell what will do it, he must try to give happiness to others. And no doubt there comes in here a frequent clash of duties. How far is he to make his neighbour happy? How far must he respect that smiling face, so easy to cloud, so hard to brighten again? And how far, on the other side, is he bound to be his brother's keeper and the prophet of his own morality? How far must he resent evil?

The difficulty is that we have little guidance; Christ's sayings on the point being hard to reconcile with each other, and (the most of them) hard to accept. But the truth of his teaching would seem to be this: in our own person and fortune, we should be ready to accept and to pardon all; it is ***our*** cheek we are to turn, ***r*** coat that we are to give away to the man who has taken ***our*** cloak. But when another's face is buffeted, perhaps a little of the lion will become us best. That we are to suffer others to be injured, and stand by, is not conceivable and surely not desirable. Revenge, says Bacon, is a kind of wild justice; its judgments at least are delivered by an insane judge; and in our own quarrel we can see nothing truly and do nothing wisely. But in the quarrel of our neighbour, let us be more bold. One person's happiness is as sacred as another's; when we cannot defend both, let us defend one with a stout heart. It is only in so far as we are doing this, that we have any right to interfere: the defence of B is our only ground of action against A. A has as good a right to go to the devil, as we to go to glory; and neither knows what he does.

The truth is that all these interventions and denunciations and militant mongerings of moral half-truths, though they be sometimes needful, though they are often enjoyable, do yet belong to an inferior grade of duties. Ill-temper and envy and revenge find here an arsenal of pious disguises; this is the playground of inverted lusts. With a little more patience and a little less temper, a gentler and wiser method might be found in almost every case; and the knot that we cut by some fine heady quarrel-scene in private life, or, in public affairs, by some denunciatory act against what we are pleased to call our neighbour's vices, might yet have been unwoven by the hand of sympathy.

IV

To look back upon the past year, and see how little we have striven and to what small purpose: and how often we have been cowardly and hung back, or temerarious and rushed unwisely in; and how every day and all day long we have transgressed the law of kindness;--it may seem a paradox, but in the bitterness of these discoveries, a certain consolation resides. Life is not designed to minister to a man's vanity. He goes upon his long business most of the time with a hanging head, and all the time like a blind child. Full of rewards and pleasures as it is--so that to see the day break or the moon rise, or to meet a friend, or to hear the dinner-call when he is hungry, fills him with surprising joys--this world is yet for him no abiding city. Friendships fall through, health fails, weariness assails him; year after year, he must thumb the hardly varying record of his own weakness and folly. It is a friendly process of detachment. When the time comes that he should go, there need be few illusions left about himself. Here lies one who meant well, tried a little, failed much:--surely that may be his epitaph, of which he need not be ashamed. Nor will he complain at the summons which calls a defeated soldier from the field: defeated, ay, if he were Paul or Marcus Aurelius!--but if there is still one inch of fight in his old spirit, undishonoured. The faith which sustained him in his life-long blindness and life-long disappointment will scarce even be required in this last formality of laying down his arms. Give him a march with his old bones; there, out of the glorious sun-coloured earth, out of the day and the dust and the ecstasy--there goes another Faithful Failure!

From a recent book of verse, where there is more than one such beautiful and manly poem, I take this memorial piece: it says better than I can, what I love to think; let it be our parting word.

"A late lark twitters from the quiet skies;
And from the west,
Where the sun, his day's work ended,
Lingers as in content,
There falls on the old, gray city
An influence luminous and serene,
A shining peace.

"The smoke ascends
In a rosy-and-golden haze. The spires
Shine, and are changed. In the valley
Shadows rise. The lark sings on. The sun,
Closing his benediction,
Sinks, and the darkening air
Thrills with a sense of the triumphing night--
Night, with her train of stars
And her great gift of sleep.

"So be my passing!
My task accomplished and the long day done,
My wages taken, and in my heart
Some late lark singing,
Let me be gathered to the quiet west,
The sundown splendid and serene,
Death."[2]

[1888.]

[Note 2: From ***A Book of Verses*** by William Ernest Henley. D. Nutt, 1888.]

The Codes Of Hammurabi And Moses QTY
W. W. Davies

The discovery of the Hammurabi Code is one of the greatest achievements of archaeology, and is of paramount interest, not only to the student of the Bible, but also to all those interested in ancient history...

Religion **ISBN: *1-59462-338-4*** **Pages:132**
MSRP ***$12.95***

The Theory of Moral Sentiments QTY
Adam Smith

This work from 1749. contains original theories of conscience amd moral judgment and it is the foundation for systemof morals.

Philosophy **ISBN: *1-59462-777-0*** **Pages:536**
MSRP ***$19.95***

Jessica's First Prayer QTY
Hesba Stretton

In a screened and secluded corner of one of the many railway-bridges which span the streets of London there could be seen a few years ago, from five o'clock every morning until half past eight, a tidily set-out coffee-stall, consisting of a trestle and board, upon which stood two large tin cans, with a small fire of charcoal burning under each so as to keep the coffee boiling during the early hours of the morning when the work-people were thronging into the city on their way to their daily toil...

Pages:84
Childrens **ISBN: *1-59462-373-2*** *MSRP* ***$9.95***

My Life and Work QTY
Henry Ford

Henry Ford revolutionized the world with his implementation of mass production for the Model T automobile. Gain valuable business insight into his life and work with his own auto-biography... "We have only started on our development of our country we have not as yet, with all our talk of wonderful progress, done more than scratch the surface. The progress has been wonderful enough but..."

Pages:300
Biographies/ **ISBN: *1-59462-198-5*** *MSRP* ***$21.95***

The Art of Cross-Examination
Francis Wellman

QTY

I presume it is the experience of every author, after his first book is published upon an important subject, to be almost overwhelmed with a wealth of ideas and illustrations which could readily have been included in his book, and which to his own mind, at least, seem to make a second edition inevitable. Such certainly was the case with me; and when the first edition had reached its sixth impression in five months, I rejoiced to learn that it seemed to my publishers that the book had met with a sufficiently favorable reception to justify a second and considerably enlarged edition. ..

Pages:412

Reference **ISBN: *1-59462-647-2*** ***MSRP $19.95***

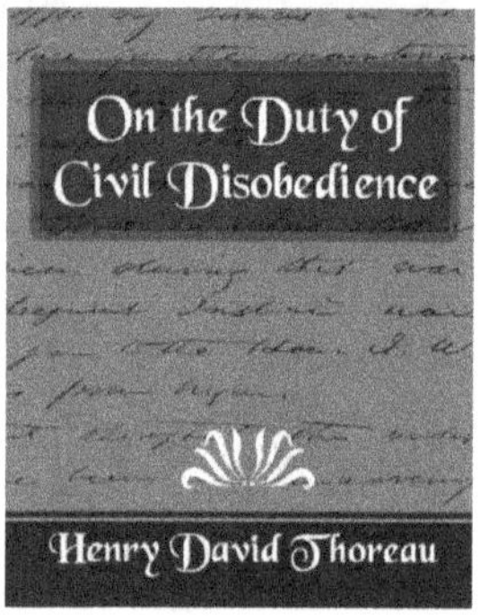

On the Duty of Civil Disobedience
Henry David Thoreau

QTY

Thoreau wrote his famous essay, On the Duty of Civil Disobedience, as a protest against an unjust but popular war and the immoral but popular institution of slave-owning. He did more than write—he declined to pay his taxes, and was hauled off to gaol in consequence. Who can say how much this refusal of his hastened the end of the war and of slavery ?

Law **ISBN: *1-59462-747-9*** **Pages:48**

MSRP $7.45

Dream Psychology Psychoanalysis for Beginners
Sigmund Freud

QTY

Sigmund Freud, born Sigismund Schlomo Freud (May 6, 1856 - September 23, 1939), was a Jewish-Austrian neurologist and psychiatrist who co-founded the psychoanalytic school of psychology. Freud is best known for his theories of the unconscious mind, especially involving the mechanism of repression; his redefinition of sexual desire as mobile and directed towards a wide variety of objects; and his therapeutic techniques, especially his understanding of transference in the therapeutic relationship and the presumed value of dreams as sources of insight into unconscious desires.

Pages:196

Psychology **ISBN: *1-59462-905-6*** ***MSRP $15.45***

The Miracle of Right Thought
Orison Swett Marden

QTY

Believe with all of your heart that you will do what you were made to do. When the mind has once formed the habit of holding cheerful, happy, prosperous pictures, it will not be easy to form the opposite habit. It does not matter how improbable or how far away this realization may see, or how dark the prospects may be, if we visualize them as best we can, as vividly as possible, hold tenaciously to them and vigorously struggle to attain them, they will gradually become actualized, realized in the life. But a desire, a longing without endeavor, a yearning abandoned or held indifferently will vanish without realization.

Pages:360

Self Help **ISBN: *1-59462-644-8*** ***MSRP $25.45***

www.bookjungle.com *email: sales@bookjungle.com fax: 630-214-0564 mail: Book Jungle PO Box 2226 Champaign, IL 61825*

QTY

The Rosicrucian Cosmo-Conception Mystic Christianity *by* ***Max Heindel*** **ISBN:** ***1-59462-188-8*** **$38.95**
The Rosicrucian Cosmo-conception is not dogmatic, neither does it appeal to any other authority than the reason of the student. It is: not controversial, but is: sent forth in the, hope that it may help to clear... *New Age/Religion Pages 646*

Abandonment To Divine Providence *by* ***Jean-Pierre de Caussade*** **ISBN:** ***1-59462-228-0*** **$25.95**
"The Rev. Jean Pierre de Caussade was one of the most remarkable spiritual writers of the Society of Jesus in France in the 18th Century. His death took place at Toulouse in 1751. His works have gone through many editions and have been republished... *Inspirational/Religion Pages 400*

Mental Chemistry *by* ***Charles Haanel*** **ISBN:** ***1-59462-192-6*** **$23.95**
Mental Chemistry allows the change of material conditions by combining and appropriately utilizing the power of the mind. Much like applied chemistry creates something new and unique out of careful combinations of chemicals the mastery of mental chemistry... *New Age Pages 354*

The Letters of Robert Browning and Elizabeth Barret Barrett 1845-1846 vol II **ISBN:** ***1-59462-193-4*** **$35.95**
by ***Robert Browning*** *and* ***Elizabeth Barrett*** *Biographies Pages 596*

Gleanings In Genesis (volume I) *by* ***Arthur W. Pink*** **ISBN:** ***1-59462-130-6*** **$27.45**
Appropriately has Genesis been termed "the seed plot of the Bible" for in it we have, in germ form, almost all of the great doctrines which are afterwards fully developed in the books of Scripture which follow... *Religion/Inspirational Pages 420*

The Master Key *by* ***L. W. de Laurence*** **ISBN:** ***1-59462-001-6*** **$30.95**
In no branch of human knowledge has there been a more lively increase of the spirit of research during the past few years than in the study of Psychology, Concentration and Mental Discipline. The requests for authentic lessons in Thought Control, Mental Discipline and... *New Age/Business Pages 422*

The Lesser Key Of Solomon Goetia *by* ***L. W. de Laurence*** **ISBN:** ***1-59462-092-X*** **$9.95**
This translation of the first book of the "Lernegton" which is now for the first time made accessible to students of Talismanic Magic was done, after careful collation and edition, from numerous Ancient Manuscripts in Hebrew, Latin, and French... *New Age/Occult Pages 92*

Rubaiyat Of Omar Khayyam *by* ***Edward Fitzgerald*** **ISBN:***1-59462-332-5* **$13.95**
Edward Fitzgerald, whom the world has already learned, in spite of his own efforts to remain within the shadow of anonymity, to look upon as one of the rarest poets of the century, was born at Bredfield, in Suffolk, on the 31st of March, 1809. He was the third son of John Purcell... *Music Pages 172*

Ancient Law *by* ***Henry Maine*** **ISBN:** ***1-59462-128-4*** **$29.95**
The chief object of the following pages is to indicate some of the earliest ideas of mankind, as they are reflected in Ancient Law, and to point out the relation of those ideas to modern thought. *Religiom/History Pages 452*

Far-Away Stories *by* ***William J. Locke*** **ISBN:** ***1-59462-129-2*** **$19.45**
"Good wine needs no bush, but a collection of mixed vintages does. And this book is just such a collection. Some of the stories I do not want to remain buried for ever in the museum files of dead magazine-numbers an author's not unpardonable vanity..." *Fiction Pages 272*

Life of David Crockett *by* ***David Crockett*** **ISBN:** ***1-59462-250-7*** **$27.45**
"Colonel David Crockett was one of the most remarkable men of the times in which he lived. Born in humble life, but gifted with a strong will, an indomitable courage, and unremitting perseverance... *Biographies/New Age Pages 424*

Lip-Reading *by* ***Edward Nitchie*** **ISBN:** ***1-59462-206-X*** **$25.95**
Edward B. Nitchie, founder of the New York School for the Hard of Hearing, now the Nitchie School of Lip-Reading, Inc, wrote "LIP-READING Principles and Practice". The development and perfecting of this meritorious work on lip-reading was an undertaking... *How-to Pages 400*

A Handbook of Suggestive Therapeutics, Applied Hypnotism, Psychic Science **ISBN:** ***1-59462-214-0*** **$24.95**
by ***Henry Munro*** *Health/New Age/Health/Self-help Pages 376*

A Doll's House: and Two Other Plays *by* ***Henrik Ibsen*** **ISBN:** ***1-59462-112-8*** **$19.95**
Henrik Ibsen created this classic when in revolutionary 1848 Rome. Introducing some striking concepts in playwriting for the realist genre, this play has been studied the world over. *Fiction/Classics/Plays 308*

The Light of Asia *by* ***sir Edwin Arnold*** **ISBN:** ***1-59462-204-3*** **$13.95**
In this poetic masterpiece, Edwin Arnold describes the life and teachings of Buddha. The man who was to become known as Buddha to the world was born as Prince Gautama of India but he rejected the worldly riches and abandoned the reigns of power when... *Religion/History/Biographies Pages 170*

The Complete Works of Guy de Maupassant *by* ***Guy de Maupassant*** **ISBN:** ***1-59462-157-8*** **$16.95**
"For days and days, nights and nights, I had dreamed of that first kiss which was to consecrate our engagement, and I knew not on what spot I should put my lips..." *Fiction/Classics Pages 240*

The Art of Cross-Examination *by* ***Francis L. Wellman*** **ISBN:** ***1-59462-309-0*** **$26.95**
Written by a renowned trial lawyer, Wellman imparts his experience and uses case studies to explain how to use psychology to extract desired information through questioning. *How-to/Science/Reference Pages 408*

Answered or Unanswered? *by* ***Louisa Vaughan*** **ISBN:** ***1-59462-248-5*** **$10.95**
Miracles of Faith in China *Religion Pages 112*

The Edinburgh Lectures on Mental Science (1909) *by* ***Thomas*** **ISBN:** ***1-59462-008-3*** **$11.95**
This book contains the substance of a course of lectures recently given by the writer in the Queen Street Hall, Edinburgh. Its purpose is to indicate the Natural Principles governing the relation between Mental Action and Material Conditions... *New Age/Psychology Pages 148*

Ayesha *by* ***H. Rider Haggard*** **ISBN:** ***1-59462-301-5*** **$24.95**
Verily and indeed it is the unexpected that happens! Probably if there was one person upon the earth from whom the Editor of this, and of a certain previous history, did not expect to hear again... *Classics Pages 380*

Ayala's Angel *by* ***Anthony Trollope*** **ISBN:** ***1-59462-352-X*** **$29.95**
The two girls were both pretty, but Lucy who was twenty-one who supposed to be simple and comparatively unattractive, whereas Ayala was credited, as her Bombwhat romantic name might show, with poetic charm and a taste for romance. Ayala when her father died was nineteen... *Fiction Pages 484*

The American Commonwealth *by* ***James Bryce*** **ISBN:** ***1-59462-286-8*** **$34.45**
An interpretation of American democratic political theory. It examines political mechanics and society from the perspective of Scotsman James Bryce *Politics Pages 572*

Stories of the Pilgrims *by* ***Margaret P. Pumphrey*** **ISBN:** ***1-59462-116-0*** **$17.95**
This book explores pilgrims religious oppression in England as well as their escape to Holland and eventual crossing to America on the Mayflower, and their early days in New England... *History Pages 268*

www.ingramcontent.com/pod-product-compliance
Lightning Source LLC
Chambersburg PA
CBHW080836250626
47160CB00008B/2958
9781438521701